P9-BYY-852

Heddy-Dale Matthias, M.D.
One Roses Bluff Parkway
Madison, MS 39110

RACHEL ISADORA

A South African Night

Greenwillow Books, New York

For Nicholas

Watercolor paints were used for the full-color art. Copyright © 1998 by Rachel Isadora Turner. All rights reserved. No part of this book may be reproduced or utilized in any form or by any means, electronic or mechanical, including photocopying, recording, or by any information storage and retrieval system, without permission in writing from the Publisher, Greenwillow Books, a division of William Morrow & Company, Inc., 1350 Avenue of the Americas, New York, NY 10019. http://www.williammorrow.com   Printed in Singapore by Tien Wah Press. First Edition 10 9 8 7 6 5 4 3 2 1   Library of Congress Cataloging-in-Publication Data.   Isadora, Rachel. A South African Night / by Rachel Isadora.   p.   cm. Summary: The inhabitants of South Africa divide their activities by day and night, as the animals in Kruger National Park go about their business while the people of Johannesburg sleep, and then lie down in the shade as the people wake up.   ISBN 0-688-11389-3 (trade).   ISBN 0-688-11390-7 (lib. bdg.)   [1. Jungle animals—Fiction.   2. Night—Fiction.   3. South Africa—Fiction.]   I. Title.   PZ7.I763So   1998   [E]—dc21   97-11203   CIP   AC

South Africa is a large country at the tip of the African continent. When the sun rises, the people awaken and begin their day. But when the sun sets, the night belongs to the animals.

It is twilight in Johannesburg. Lights go on in the city. Stores close for the night.

Children go home after a long day.

It is time for bed.

But more than two hundred miles away, in Kruger National Park, the animals begin to stir.

A black mamba snake raises his head and watches for his next meal.

Lionesses leave their cubs to hunt for food.

A hungry leopard moves
from the shadows of
the bush to find his prey.

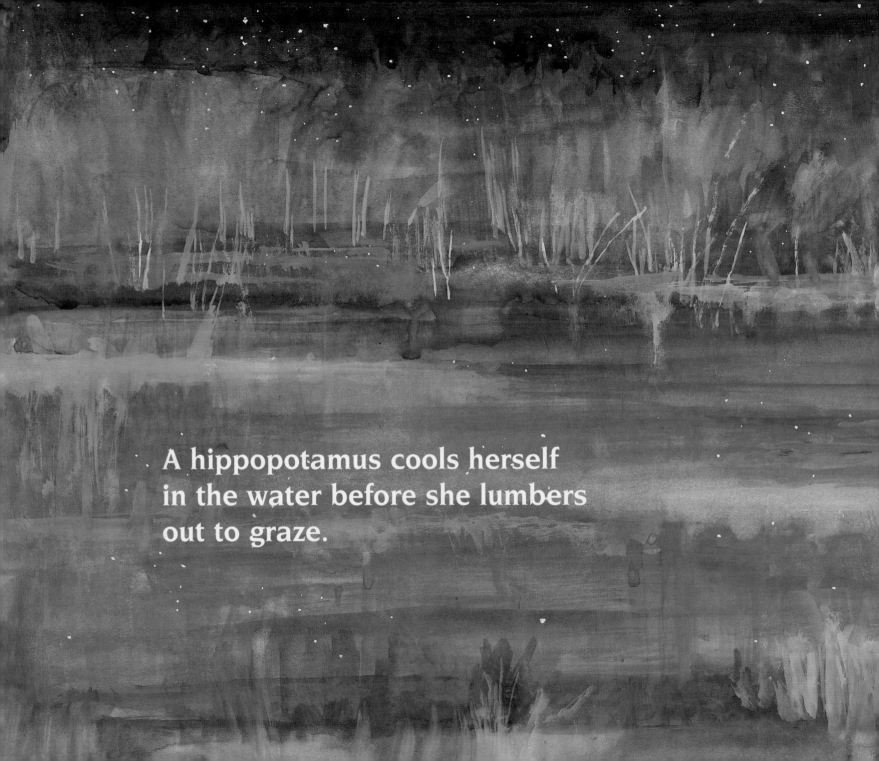

A hippopotamus cools herself
in the water before she lumbers
out to graze.

An elephant brings her baby
to the water hole to drink.

After the long night, the sun rises
and the animals lie down in the shade
to sleep.

And in
Johannesburg,
the people
wake up to
a new day.